COMMANDER IN CHEESE

The Birthday Suit

To James F. Brown—a man so humble,
he forgets his own birthday

Text copyright © 2017 by Lindsey Leavitt, LLC
Cover art and interior illustrations copyright © 2017 by A. G. Ford

Photo permissions pp. 94–99 president portraits, p. 105 General Washington, p. 107 Lady Bird Johnson gown from the collection of the Library of Congress Prints and Photographs Division online at loc.org, p. 101 Ronald Reagan courtesy of the Reagan Library.

Visit us on the Web!
SteppingStonesBooks.com
randomhousekids.com

Educators and librarians, for a variety of teaching tools, visit us at RHTeachersLibrarians.com

Library of Congress Cataloging-in-Publication Data is available upon request.
ISBN 978-1-101-93121-9 (trade)—ISBN 978-1-101-93122-6 (lib. bdg.)—
ISBN 978-1-101-93123-3 (ebook)

Printed in the United States of America
10 9 8 7 6 5 4 3 2 1

This book has been officially leveled by using the
F&P Text Level Gradient™ Leveling System.

COMMANDER IN CHEESE
The Birthday Suit

4

Lindsey Leavitt • illustrated by A. G. Ford

A STEPPING STONE BOOK™

Random House 🏠 New York

Mice don't have a good history when it comes to surprises. Here's a list of reasons why:

1. Mousetraps
2. Pest control
3. Predators
4. Fire

Of course, these are all *bad* surprises. Sometimes mice have good surprises. Like when the baker makes a small mistake. Those treats go into the trash. This means it's sugar time for the Squeakertons, a mouse family that has eaten White House food for over two hundred years.

And birthdays! Birthdays are the best way to surprise somebody. Mr. James F. Squeakerton, the sort-of mouse president, asked his wife, Vivian, to marry him on her birthday. She got to smash open a piñata. Inside, she found candy *and* a wedding ribbon. (Mice don't wear rings on their claws. That would be weird.)

The Squeakerton mice have a very special celebration planned on Presidents' Day. Presidents' Day falls on a different day every year, and this year, it happens to be on Gregory Squeakerton's birthday. Gregory is the bodyguard for James F. Squeakerton's children, Ava and Dean. Gregory makes sure those little mice stay out of trouble. Most of the time.

Something else you should know about Gregory: he loves history. He is very proud to live in the White House. He can tell you anything you want to know about the White House. Probably even things you don't want to know. Like, did you know it takes 570 gallons of paint to cover the White House? See? Not a very useful fact (unless you're a painter).

Yes, the Squeakerton family wanted to celebrate the wonderful leaders they'd watched throughout the years. But they also really wanted to make the day unforgettable for Gregory.

There were just three problems:

1. Mice like Gregory don't like surprises. Gregory plans out his whole day, from his breakfast menu to his bathroom breaks. There's no room for surprises in his schedule.

2. C-a-t-s *love* surprises. They also love messing up surprises for other animals. C-a-t-s are evil. You probably already knew that, but mice think it's important to remind you.

3. Humans run the show in the White House. And sometimes human plans mess up mouse plans. Not that humans have any idea about that. Those guys really only pay attention to themselves.

2

"Libby, have you ever tasted red velvet cake?" Dean Squeakerton asked the cook as he bit on the end of his pen.

Libby set down a pan. "No. We've never had that for leftovers."

Mice were very good at finding "leftovers." Some was in the trash. Lots of food was left right on the plates! Mice thought guests got so nervous to meet the president that they didn't eat their food.

Which was perfect for the mice.

"What do you think about this?" Dean asked. He held up a picture.

His sister, Ava, frowned. "Are those all cupcakes?"

Dean shrugged. "Yeah. So?"

"How are you going to make the Lincoln Memorial out of cupcakes?" Ava asked. "How big is that supposed to be?"

"Only ten feet tall."

Libby snorted. "You're a creative mouse. But you need to think smaller."

Dean didn't like thinking smaller. He was small enough already. Dean wanted to be an architect when he grew up. He wanted to build buildings that touched the sky, with plenty of secret rooms for the mice.

"We haven't had cake in so long," Ava said. "I'm excited. I hope it's carrot cake. I love carrots. Or lemon! Or chocolate. Never mind, I love *all* cake."

"We'll be lucky if we find one cupcake," Libby said. "A ten-foot memorial is not going to happen."

"You just need more imagination," Dean said.

"Imagination about what?" Gregory bounced into the kitchen.

Dean shoved his picture under the table. Of

course, Gregory didn't know about their surprise birthday plans. If he did, it wouldn't be a surprise.

"Dean wants to build a new Liberty Bell." Ava took her brother's tail. "It's an . . . extra-credit project. For school."

Gregory popped a seed into his mouth. "That's great that you're working together. You know, 'We cannot build our own future without—' "

" 'Helping others to build theirs,' " Ava and Dean said. It was the same President Bill Clinton quote they'd heard a million times. They had heard a million quotes a million times.

"Well, little mice, I have big plans for us today!" Gregory said. "I've prepared a Presidents' Day packet. Very interesting stuff. I thought we could start by memorizing the presidents' birthdays."

"Um, Gregory . . . ," Ava said.

"Then we'll read the top-ten speeches." Gregory started to pace. "Next, I'll record the Presidents' Day surprise activities planned in the East Room. In fact, we should meet after to discuss what we learned. . . ."

"Wait, it's Presidents' Day today?" Dean asked. Of course he already knew this. Presidents' Day was always the third Monday of February. The Squeakerton siblings had been preparing for this day for a very long time. But they couldn't let *Gregory* know that.

Gregory almost choked on his seed. "What? What? Yes! It's Presidents' Day. It's one of the *most* important days of the year, besides the Fourth of July or Election Day. Can you believe this, Libby?"

Libby shook her head. "I forgot too. I'm still doing dishes from our Valentine's Day dinner."

"Unbelievable," Gregory mumbled.

"Well, we have to go," Ava said. "Since we're off from school today, Dean and I are going to do more . . . of that extra-credit project. Together. If we have time after, we can do some of your president stuff."

"Well . . . yes. You know today . . . is also very important to me." Gregory fixed his tie.

Ava wanted to hug him and shout "Happy birthday!" right then, but they couldn't give away the surprise. Surprises are slippery like that. Sometimes you have to be a little mean before you can be very nice.

This is also why some *humans* don't like surprises.

"We know you love your presidents!" Ava smiled. "Yay for Presidents' Day. We're just going to check on something, and then you can tell us what cake President Franklin Pierce liked."

"He liked fried apple pie," Gregory mumbled.

It would have been much easier to throw a regular birthday party for Gregory, especially since he already seemed sad that no one remembered. But they couldn't ruin the fun now, not when everyone had worked so hard.

Libby served Gregory some leftover Valentine's chocolate.

"I like your bow," Gregory said.

"Thank you," Libby said. "Did you want to tell me some facts to make you feel better?"

"Yes. Did you know President Polk and President Harding have the same birthday? November second."

Dean rolled up his cupcake design and hurried out of the room with Ava.

"This isn't going to be easy," Ava said. "At least we get to eat cake at the end."

Dean rubbed his forehead. "'If you can't stand the heat, get out of the kitchen.' President Truman said that."

"What does that mean?" Ava asked.

"I don't know. That we need to get out of here, I guess."

They really did have a project they were working on, hidden in a small corner of the Treasure Rooms. When they finished, the birthday surprise countdown would begin.

Dean pulled a notebook out of his pocket. Inside was a list . . .

1. Talk to Libby about a birthday cake.
2. Check on Gregory's birthday suit.
3. Distract Gregory for a few hours.
4. Trick Gregory into coming to his party.
5. SURPRISE!

Dean crossed off list item number one. It was too bad Libby couldn't make that ten-foot cupcake memorial, but he was sure she would make something special. She liked Gregory. Sometimes Dean wondered if Libby *like* liked Gregory.

"Ready for the next part?" Ava asked.

"Of course," Dean said.

Mice are very good planners. The reason mice are so good at planning is because they understand that everyone needs to have a different job. Gregory was a bodyguard who shared way too many facts. Aunt Agnes was in charge of the entire mouse tech world. Mr. James F. Squeakerton was the leader of the family.

And Cousin Sullivan was a tailor. He made sure everyone had the right clothes to do the job they needed to do. He made bow ties for Mr. Squeakerton and overalls for Agnes.

Sullivan Squeakerton was waiting for the mice in the Treasure Rooms. Sullivan was what humans call a teenager. Dean and Ava were still trying to figure out what exactly a teenager was. They'd seen human teenagers in the White House before. But mice teenagers . . . they were different.

Mice teenagers got very, very excited about everything. All the time. They could be hard to talk to sometimes.

Sullivan was already inside the Wheel. You know those wheels that gerbils or hamsters run around in? The rodent just spins and spins for no reason. The mice had made one of these just for teenage mice. The rest of the mice—kids and adults—thought it was a waste of time, but whatever.

"Hey, guys!" Sullivan sang. That's another thing. Sullivan didn't say words. He sang them. "So fantastic to see you!"

"Is it ready?" Dean asked.

"Sure is, sure is! And it is so rad! The rad-
dest ever!"

"Sulley, can you get off that wheel?" Ava
asked. "You're making us dizzy."

"Sure!" Sullivan hopped down and did a
cartwheel. Just to show off. Ava and Dean were

not excited to turn into teenagers someday. "Right this way, right this way!"

The Treasure Rooms were a bunch of mouse rooms hidden inside the walls of the White House. There was a Stuff We Use Collection, a Cooking Tools Collection, even a History of Cheese Collection.

The Fabric Collection was Ava's favorite room. She would slip inside just to rub her claw against all the amazing pieces of clothing. Here are Ava's four favorite items . . .

1. Hats, especially that aviator hat
2. Scarves, glorious, long scarves
3. Beads, beautiful beads
4. The Secret Suit

"It's amazing!" Ava squeaked when she saw the black suit. Sullivan had really outdone himself with this one. Gregory wore a suit every single day. Sullivan had borrowed one of these suits and remade it into an Abraham Lincoln costume.

Gregory adored presidents, of course. But there were three presidents he adored most: Abraham Lincoln, Thomas Jefferson, and Chester A. Arthur.

1. Abraham Lincoln: He made sure all
   Americans were free! Mice were fans
   of freedom.
2. Thomas Jefferson: Ever heard of the
   Declaration of Independence? Gregory
   had it memorized.
3. Chester A. Arthur: This one was a
   mystery. Dean thought it had
   something to do with the strange
   beard.

So they made Gregory a birthday suit to look like his favorite president.

"Gregory is a very large mouse! So large!" Sullivan hopped from one foot to the other. "Are you sure he's not a gerbil?"

"He's not a gerbil," Dean said.

"Same size as a gerbil," Sullivan said. "But I still got it done. I added some fun parts too. There are glasses in the pocket. And look!" Sullivan opened the suit jacket. "If Gregory pushes this button, it shoots water into someone's face. Like a clown."

"Gregory hates clowns," Dean said. "And just about anything funny."

"Well, then I guess it's good I didn't add the pie shooter." Sullivan shrugged. "But look at the bow tie!"

Sullivan tugged on the sides of the bow tie. A laser beam appeared.

Ava squinted. "I think Gregory would rather have facts taped inside his jacket than lasers coming out of his tie."

"Humans love lasers. They chase them like dogs chase c-a-t-s," Sullivan said. "And Gregory can keep his facts in his hat."

"The laser is cool!" Dean said. "Can you do that to my shirt?"

"You're still little mice," Sullivan said, even though he wasn't much older than them. "We don't do special things to your clothes until you have a special job."

"So you'll make me a flight jacket when I become a pilot?" Ava asked.

Sullivan hopped back on the wheel. "If that happens!"

"*When* it happens," Ava corrected.

The kids were very excited about the hidden

gadgets. They wondered if any other mice they knew had special details in their clothes.

"Can we at least get some cool clothes because we're planning this whole surprise?" Dean asked. "Like surprise ninja clothes?"

"No time!" Sullivan wheezed. "I have to run around this wheel two thousand more times before the party."

"Why?" Ava asked.

"Because! Because!" Sullivan said.

It didn't make much sense, but that's a teenager for you.

Dean pulled out his list and crossed off number two. "Time for the next job."

"Great. Let's go spy on some humans," Ava said.

"We're getting everything done so fast," Dean said.

Ava nodded. "Yep. We'll be eating delicious cake very soon. Nothing is going wrong!"

It was true. Nothing had gone wrong.

Yet.

Washington, D.C., was a great place to visit on Presidents' Day. Visitors could walk to the Lincoln Memorial or the Washington Monument. They could tour the many amazing museums. Some people even dressed up like old presidents and went to parties or parades.

This was President Caroline Abbey's first Presidents' Day in the White House. She'd decided to do something special. The mice didn't yet know what that special thing was.

Gregory was already in the doorway of the

mouse hole in the East Room. He had the camera strapped on him so he could record everything for other mice watching in the Situation Room. Gregory took his job very seriously. Gregory took everything seriously.

Dean patted Gregory on the back. "Gregory, we have a surprise for you."

Gregory didn't even turn around. "I hate surprises."

"Gregory, look," Ava said.

Gregory turned around and squeaked.

Ava and Dean held up the new suit. "Ta-da!"

"It's beautiful!" Gregory touched the fabric. "Is this a birthday present?"

This was the biggest clue Gregory had given about his birthday. Dean ignored it. "Abraham Lincoln's birthday was a few days ago, so I guess you can call it that."

Again, it is really hard to pretend that you don't know about a birthday.

"But . . . why did you make this?" Gregory asked.

"Dad said you needed to dress up for the . . . Presidents' Day activities," Ava said. "It's part of your job."

Gregory nodded. "Then it's an order. I'll go change. Be right back."

"Why would Dad make him wear an Abraham Lincoln costume just to watch some humans?" Dean asked his sister.

"No clue. I made it up." Ava frowned. "I don't like the lying part of the surprise."

Gregory reappeared. The suit fit him perfectly. He even had on the fake beard. That part looked a little silly, but Ava and Dean would never tell Gregory that.

"I'm on camera duty today," Gregory said. "The big event they have planned looks like it involves schoolchildren. Stay close. This could be dangerous."

Ava and Dean weren't worried about schoolchildren. They already knew the president's kids, Banks and Macey. And Banks and Macey even knew about the little mice. They weren't exactly friends, but they were at least friendly.

Ava counted fifty-five kids lined up in the White House East Room. The East Room is where state dinners and balls are held, so it is very large. Most of the kids kept looking up at the ceiling. People do that with high ceilings. Have you ever noticed that?

Each student was dressed as a president or First Lady. The mini Grace Coolidge looked pretty in her flapper gown. Ava wondered if she could get Sullivan to make her a dress like that someday.

There were also a lot of presidents dressed in suits, although some had on knee breeches. Kid James Monroe had on a very nice wig.

"Isn't it beautiful?" Gregory wiped away a tear. "Look at all these children so excited about their country's history."

"This seems like a really big school project," Ava said.

"Lots of schools in the country do a presidential fair," Gregory said. "See those posters? It looks like these students are present-ing those today. The difference is they'll share

their schoolwork with the current president of the United States. Best field trip ever."

"Thank you so much for coming today!" A woman stood in front of the children. She had on a purple skirt and a tired smile. "The president will be with you in just a moment. She's on the phone with Chad."

"Who is Chad?" Dean whispered.

"It's a country," Gregory whispered. "Now stop talking."

"While we're waiting for the president, we have another special guest," the woman said. "Meet Clover!"

The mice all groaned.

Clover, the president's c-a-t, walked out in a George Washington costume. Clover once did a

presidential fashion show in the West Wing that ended when the fire sprinklers got everyone wet. It was a bad day for Clover but obviously didn't spoil her love for dressing up. Dressing up got her attention.

Clover *loved* attention. She meowed with delight as the children cheered.

The girl dressed like Bill Clinton waved. "We had a cat named Socks when I was president. Can I pet Clover?"

"I want to pet him too!" President Zachary

Taylor said. Or the kid dressed like Zachary Taylor.

The lady in the purple skirt held up her hand. "If we all pet Clover, we would do nothing else all day. Instead, Clover will walk around and check out each of your displays. Just like General Washington observing his troops!"

"I can't believe Clover gets to dress up *and* read all those reports," Gregory said. "That is my dream, and a c-a-t gets to do it? We should just go."

Ava glanced at the clock. They were supposed to keep Gregory here for two hours. They had to keep him away from the kitchen, the hallways, the Treasure Rooms . . . anywhere he might spot a mouse preparing for his party.

"Do you want to walk around?" Ava asked.

"How?" Gregory asked. "I'm wearing an

Abraham Lincoln suit and holding a camera. These kids would scream if they saw me."

This was true, which was silly. Mice were just as cute as c-a-t-s, but humans seemed to be very scared of them.

"This is a big deal for you," Dean said. "We don't want you to miss it. There has to be a way to get you out there, Gregory."

There was. But it wasn't easy. It never was.

Dean and Ava put their heads together. They thought of one way they could get Gregory closer to the reports. It was bad. They thought of another idea. It was worse. Then they thought of an idea that might not be the worst idea ever, which was better than nothing.

The tables were in a large circle. Kids stood in front of their presidential posters. A circular couch was in the middle of the room.

The couch was like an island, and all the carpet was an ocean. The mice had to cross the carpet to get to the island, where they could hide under the cushion.

No one ever said it was a *good* plan. Just not the worst idea ever.

"Gregory, this suit is special," Ava said. "If you pull on your bow tie, it shoots a laser."

"Why would I want to do that?" Gregory asked.

"So we can distract the kids and get over to that couch," Dean said.

"Do you know how dangerous that is?" Gregory asked.

"Oh, boy," Ava said. "Here we go."

"We could be stepped on. Or trampled! One of those kids could throw a heavy object at us. The Secret Service could trap us. We could ruin everything for all the Squeakertons!"

Ava looked at the clock. They still had an

hour and forty-five minutes to distract Gregory. He was not an easy mouse to distract.

"Gregory, do you want to read the reports?" Ava asked.

"And see the kids' costumes up close?" Dean asked.

"Of course I do!" Gregory cried. "History on display! In my favorite room!"

"Then pull. Now!" Ava said.

Gregory closed his eyes and pulled on his bow tie. A laser shot across the room. It was amazing how big the beam was, coming from a mouse-sized outfit. Sullivan might be a weird teenager, but he knew how to design a suit.

"Look at that red laser!" kid Nancy Reagan shouted. By the way, Nancy's favorite color was red. Humans think mice can't see red, but that's because mice want humans to think that.

"Is someone spying on us?" kid Richard Nixon asked. "Should we hide our reports?"

The kids did not look where the laser was coming *from,* only where it was pointing. They laughed as the laser bounced around the room.

The laser was bouncing because Gregory was running.

Mice are very smart. Humans? Eh.

The mice made it to the couch and slid underneath the seat of the cushion.

"Aw, the laser is gone," one of the kids said.

"Check the pocket," Dean told Gregory. "There are glasses in there."

Gregory pulled out the glasses, which also

worked as binoculars. He started to read the reports.

"Oh, this is so interesting!" Gregory said. "Did you know Benjamin Harrison was afraid of electricity? He wouldn't touch a light switch! I can see why. It was new at the time. Good to be safe . . ."

The kids wandered from poster to poster, eating treats from different periods in history. Dean really wished he could have some of the cheese wheel served at kid Andrew Jackson's display. Ava wanted to nibble on the johnnycake served by kid John Adams.

Macey and Banks walked over to the other side of the couch and sat down. The mice tried not to think what would have happened if the Abbey kids had sat on them instead.

"This is weird." Banks rubbed his fake

Rutherford B. Hayes beard. "We're on a field trip *in our house*."

"It's America's house," Macey said. She was dressed like President Dwight D. Eisenhower. The bald cap itched her head. "I've heard that ten times today."

"Jesse Wong keeps asking to go into my room!" Banks slumped against the seat. "I have a Lego tower in there that's only half done. I don't want anyone to see it."

"Mrs. Pena asked me if I could get her into the Oval Office," Macey said. "I don't want to take my teacher to my mom's job!"

"Why did Mom do this?" Banks asked.

"I think she's trying to be a regular mom," Macey said. "But how many regular moms invite both of their kids' classes to their house?"

Banks stood up. "Maybe next time we can just . . . play. With friends. Like two."

"Two friends who will treat us *normally*," Macey agreed.

"How are we going to tell Mom that?" Banks asked.

Macey groaned. "I don't know. I feel like

everyone is watching us here. More than I already feel that way."

"Let's just keep showing off Clover," Banks said. "At least she loves it."

Ava and Dean stayed quiet until the human kids left.

"I feel bad," Ava said.

"I do too," Dean said.

"I don't!" Gregory said. "They live in the most important house in this country. It's an honor. Now listen. There is so much more to learn!"

Gregory kept reading off more and more facts. He read for thirty minutes. This was good because it meant Ava and Dean only had to distract Gregory for another hour or so. This was also bad because the little mice were about ready to fall asleep.

Then music started playing. The song was

"Hail to the Chief," which of course meant the president was walking into the room.

The kids scrambled back to their displays. Kid John Quincy Adams almost tripped on his coattails.

"Thank you so much for coming!" President Caroline Abbey said. "I know you worked hard on these posters. I've wanted Macey and Banks to bring their classmates here since I took office. Doesn't my son look handsome dressed like President Hayes?"

Banks blushed so red it showed through his fake beard. "Mommmm, you're embarrassing me."

"Right, right, sorry." President Abbey cleared her throat. "Anyway, you all look so presidential. I'm going to visit every single display. Clover will come with me. Then I'll give you a private White House tour before we bring reporters in to take photos."

"I would *love* to hear the students give their reports!" Gregory sighed. "That Clover is so lucky."

Dean yawned. "Oh, well. You aren't a c-a-t, Gregory. You're a mouse in an Abraham Lincoln costume. Now the next question is, how are we going to get back to the mouse hole?"

Gregory smiled. "We'll worry about that in a few hours."

"A few *hours*?" Ava asked.

"Yes, of course. We can't go running around when the president is out there. No, no. I'm happy to stay here until all the kids leave and the staff cleans the entire room. That should be around seven tonight." Gregory patted his coat. "Did you kids pack any snacks in this suit?"

Snacks reminded Ava of the cake she wasn't going to eat now. It was probably carrot cake too, her favorite.

"I think this is what they call a *backfire*," Dean whispered to his sister.

6

Here's the good news:

1. Dean and Ava talked to Libby about the cake.
2. They got Gregory a birthday suit.
3. They kept Gregory busy for almost an hour.
4. They were safe under a couch cushion.

Here's the not-so-good news:

1. They were stuck in the middle of a room.

2. With a bunch of kids in costumes.

3. Gregory wasn't going to leave until seven.

4. The surprise party started at three.

5. There was a c-a-t nearby.

"Gregory, we can't stay here that long," Ava said. "We have to get back soon."

"Why?" Gregory said. "There's nothing else special happening today, right?"

Dean blew out a breath. Surprise parties were *so hard*. "We are under a cushion. The Abbey kids almost sat on us already."

Gregory shrugged. "Unless you can come up with a better plan, we wait here."

And so they waited. And waited. They waited another forty minutes while the president walked around to each display. Gregory stayed quiet so he could hear some of the conversation.

Dean fell asleep. Ava kicked him when he snored.

Finally, the president said, "And now, students, please follow your teachers while we tour more of the White House."

"Look with your eyes, not with your hands!" a teacher called.

Macey and Banks were the last ones out of the room. They didn't need to tour the White House. They had seen it plenty.

"Dean! Dean! Let's go!" Ava pushed the cushion off the couch. "We have twenty minutes to get you-know-where."

"I didn't hear anything from President Polk," Gregory said. "I love Polk!"

Ava took his hand. "I know. But we need to go now, Gregory. Remember all that stuff you told us about danger?"

The mice scrambled down the couch and into

the middle of the floor. Dean and Ava could see the mouse hole! They would get Gregory to his party just in time. The plan could still work.

But Gregory was not in a hurry to leave. Gregory was in a trance. He had learned so many facts, and he wanted more.

Gregory wandered over to the Polk display and started reading. Ava tried grabbing one hand. Dean grabbed another. They couldn't pull him. Gregory was a very, very large and strong mouse.

"Gregory . . . Gregory!" Ava breathed. "We . . . want to show you something."

"Sure, in a bit. I want to read about Polk's early years first."

Ava and Dean tugged at Gregory. The camera came off his back.

"Sorry. I forgot where I was for a moment." Gregory shook his head. "Look, there is a bowl

of Tennessee-shaped pins on the James K. Polk table. Let me just grab one for the Treasure Rooms."

Footsteps clicked down the hall. Ava and Dean bolted for the mouse hole. Dean had to drag the camera across the floor. Gregory grabbed a pin and ran.

Ava and Dean made it in safe.

Gregory, however, did not.

"It's a gerbil!" Kid Nancy Reagan bent down

and scooped up Gregory. "It's an adorable gerbil dressed up like Abraham Lincoln. And he's
holding a pin! I came back to get my purse, and
I found the cutest pet ever!"

Ava and Dean watched in terror. This was
definitely a day of surprises but not the good
kind.

"How are we going to save him?" Ava asked
her brother.

"Did you see that?" Dean asked. "If she saw
a mouse, she would have screamed. She only
picked up Gregory because she thought he was
a gerbil. Gerbils aren't cute!"

"Dean, focus!" Ava said.

Kid Nancy Reagan was already walking
back to join the tour. "I'm going to show you
to all my friends! Maybe we can dress you up
some more."

Gregory had always wanted a presidential

tour of the White House. This was *not* how he wanted it to happen, though.

In fact, this tour might be the last thing Gregory got to see.

Ever!

Sullivan and Aunt Agnes met Dean and Ava at the mouse hole within seconds. Sullivan had on tight black clothes.

"We saw!" Aunt Agnes said, totally out of breath. "On the camera! I can't believe they got Gregory."

"Why didn't he use the hidden sword in the leg of his pants?" Sullivan asked.

"Probably because he didn't know!" Dean said. "You hid a *sword* in there?"

"We need a plan," Agnes said firmly. "We are mice. We always need a plan."

The mice tapped their heads, hoping an idea would come. Ava and Dean felt like they'd used all their ideas for the day already.

"They'll be on the tour for a bit. Let's head back to the Treasure Rooms and see if we can think of something," Aunt Agnes said.

The mice marched down the hall. Gregory wouldn't be hurt. Probably. Kids don't hurt animals they think are pets. Still, it was a scary situation to be in. And how on earth would anyone explain the suit?

Dean opened the door to the Treasure Rooms.

"Surprise!" the entire Squeakerton colony cheered. Confetti fell to the floor.

Dean grabbed at his chest.

His sister pushed past him. "False alarm."

Sullivan hopped up and down. "Nancy Reagan took Gregory! He's gone forever! Gone forever!"

The other mice just blinked at Sullivan. He was a teenager. Teenagers always got too excited.

Ava and Dean's mom ran up and gave them a hug. She wore a straw hat and white shirt. Vivian Squeakerton was a botanist. She worked in the garden and always smelled like sunshine and roses. "Your dad is on the radio with a mouse colony in Peru. He'll be here soon. Tell us what happened."

So Ava and Dean did. When they finished, Ava said, "They have to go back to the East Room soon to meet the reporters. So we only have a few minutes to decide on a plan."

Sullivan jumped up and down. "I got it! I'm going to run into the room and shoot sleeping gas everywhere. The humans will all fall asleep, that girl will drop Gregory, and—boom!—we're free. Okay, here I go!"

Aunt Agnes gently grabbed his arm. "Son, hold on."

"Mom, I know what I'm doing," Sullivan said.

"Mice need a *careful* plan," Agnes said. "If you run out there with sleeping gas, Gregory is going to fall asleep too. So are you."

"Where did he get sleeping gas?" Dean whispered. Sullivan had so many tricks up his sleeve.

Sullivan stopped bouncing. "Okay, okay, let me think. Let me think!"

Vivian Squeakerton took her daughter's hand. "I know that face, darling. You have a plan."

"I do." Ava smiled. "The first thing we need to do is talk to Clover."

"*Clover?*" Sullivan fell over. "You can't talk to a c-a-t!"

"We already have," Dean said. "One time. Outside the Treasure Rooms."

The mice in the room gasped. No mouse had ever talked to a c-a-t. Well, no *living* mouse, at least.

"But what if she eats you?" Mrs. Squeakerton asked.

"She won't. She only eats fish," Ava said. "She told us."

"Do you think Clover will help us?" her mom asked.

"I don't know," Ava said. "But it's worth a try."

Mrs. Squeakerton nodded. Usually it would be Gregory talking to them about this. Gregory would tell them all the dangers. It was weird that Gregory got caught because he was not being a smart and careful mouse. Weird and scary.

"All right," Mrs. Squeakerton said. "Be brave, little mice."

"What should they take with them?" Agnes asked.

"I know!" Sulley scrambled out of the room. He returned with two green hats.

"Do these have X-ray glasses inside?" Dean asked.

"Or do they have a built-in headset?" Ava asked.

"No!" Sullivan said. "Green berets are worn by US Army Special Forces. President John F. Kennedy said they are a mark of distinction."

"But what do they *do*?" Dean asked.

Sullivan rolled his eyes. "They remind you to be brave! Not everything has to be spy gear. Sometimes clothes are just clothes, okay?"

Ava and Dean stuck the berets on their heads and hurried to the East Room with Aunt Agnes.

"I'm going to use the camera to record from the door of the mouse hole," Aunt Agnes said. "We'll send in troops if you need it."

"Sending in troops" is always the last move for mice. The staff would know there were mice in the house. It would mean exterminators and mouse traps everywhere. So the best idea was for Gregory to come back on his own.

The room echoed with the whispers and footsteps of fifty-five schoolchildren returning from their tour.

"I want to pet the gerbil!" kid Millard Fillmore said.

"No, I'm next!" kid George W. Bush said.

Clover slunk into the room, her tail dragging. Her George Washington wig slumped to the side. No one was fighting to pet *her* anymore.

A circle formed around kid Nancy Reagan. When a teacher walked into the room, Nancy hid Gregory behind her back. She had a new pet, and she wasn't about to give it up.

Ava and Dean slid out of the mouse hole. Clover was next to the Gerald Ford poster. They waited until the nearby kids were looking away before hurrying over.

Clover took one look at them and growled.

"Why are you rodents wearing those stupid hats?" Clover asked.

"So we can be brave," Dean said. "We

want to make a deal with you. It's our friend Gregory's birthday today."

"And we're throwing him a surprise party," Ava said.

"Just because I was nice to you in private does not mean I will be nice now," Clover said. "Why do you need me for a surprise party?"

"Obviously we can't throw Gregory a party now that kid Nancy Reagan mouse-napped him."

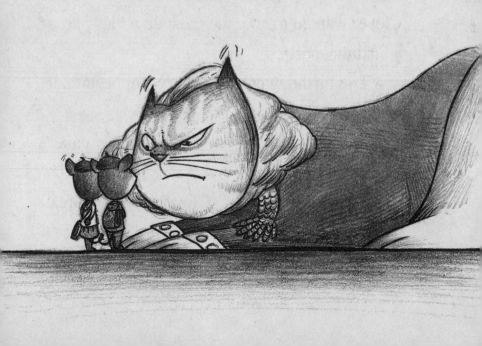

"That gerbil in the Abe Lincoln costume is a mouse?" Clover asked.

"Yes. He's our friend," Ava said.

Clover narrowed her eyes. "What's in it for me?"

"We'll tell all the mice that you're very nice," Dean offered.

"Nope." Clover yawned. "I want the birthday cake. All of it."

Dean and Ava looked at each other. Ava had been waiting for cake for weeks! Of course Clover wanted to take the most delicious part of a birthday party.

"The birthday cake is a very important part of the surprise," Ava said.

"And it's hard for our cook to get a cake!" Dean said.

"You have a cook?" Clover asked. "Great. She owes me a free dinner too."

"No way," Ava said. "Gregory loves cake! We all do."

"Ava," Dean said. "Think about it."

Ava did. They had to do what Clover wanted. They were lucky that she didn't eat mice. She *spoke* Mouse. She might not be the nicest animal ever, but what did they expect? They were dealing with a c-a-t.

And if they didn't get Gregory back, there wouldn't be a party anyway. Ava had to give up on her cake dreams for his sake.

"Okay, we'll give you the cake," Ava said.

Clover purred. "Excellent. I would have done it anyway, but this is the icing on the cake!"

"Hey!" Ava said. "Why are you so sneaky?"

"Because I'm a cat." Clover licked her paw. "Now let's get that gerbil out of here. He's stealing my spotlight."

8

Ava and Dean squeezed under Clover's George Washington wig. It was smelly and fuzzy under there, but they knew better than to complain.

Clover tried to get close to the circle of kids, but they kept pushing her away.

"Don't let the cat near the gerbil," kid John Tyler said. "He'll eat it!"

"He?" Clover spat. "I am not a *he*! And I would never eat a mouse. They're disgusting."

"Thank you," Ava whispered. "We're glad you think so."

"Now what do I do?" Clover said.

Macey noticed Clover outside of the group and scooped her up. "Hey there, kitty. Are they ignoring you?"

Clover meowed.

"Well, I know the feeling," Macey said. "Here, I'll scratch the top of your head. You love that."

She lifted the top of the wig. Dean and Ava grabbed for the wig, but it was too late. Macey already saw them.

For other mice with other humans, this could have been very awful. The mice were lucky that

Macey was the human that found them. Very lucky.

"Clover, why are there two mice under your wig?" Macey asked.

Clover meowed. Seriously, what else could Clover do right then?

Ava waved. Seriously, what else could Ava do right then?

"Okay, I'm going to put the wig back on. I'm guessing that the Abe Lincoln gerbil is your friend. I don't know why they keep calling him a gerbil. He's obviously a large mouse."

Exactly!

Macey petted Clover's fur. "That's really nice of you to help these little mice. When everyone finally leaves today, I'll play ball with you, okay?"

Clover meowed again. Dean figured if you had to be a pet, at least be a pet with a nice owner. He wondered if he could ever be friends with the human girl. He laughed. A mouse and a human—friends? Can you imagine?

Just then, the president marched into the room, followed by a dozen people with cameras.

"Did everyone enjoy the tour?" she asked.

Ava and Dean stood on Clover's head and pulled back the wig so they could see what was happening. The kids shuffled into a line. They all looked guilty.

The kids nodded. Then kid James Monroe blurted out, "Nancy Reagan found a gerbil!"

Ava and Dean groaned.

"Can I see?" President Abbey asked.

Nancy Reagan took her hands from behind her back. Gregory was a little wrinkled, but when he saw the president, he stood up tall.

"He's darling!" The president clapped her hands together. "Is that an Abe Lincoln suit?"

Gregory saluted.

"Did he just *salute*?" Clover asked.

"Gregory loves presidents," Dean said. "This is a big honor for him."

"*I'm* supposed to get more attention," Clover said. "This is not getting me more attention."

"Clover!" the president called. "Come over here for some pictures. Today is Presidents' Day, and here we have the two presidents we celebrate!"

"Mom will freak if she sees those mice, Clover," Macey whispered. "She's fine with gerbils, not mice."

Seriously, does this one-rodent-is-okay-but-not-the-other rule make sense to anyone?

The press snapped picture after picture of Clover and Gregory. Ava and Dean had to stay under the smelly wig. Finally, the president said, "I want to thank the students of Apollo Intermediate School for presenting their president reports today. I learned a lot of interesting facts.

Many people think Abraham Lincoln once said, 'Whatever you are, be a good one.' You all were very good presidents today, and I am honored to be with you. Thank you."

The press applauded, and the students beamed. President Abbey hadn't been president for very long, but she was getting good at speeches.

"Now, let's get a picture with the gerbil's owner!" President Abbey said. "Nancy Reagan, do you want to come and get in the picture?"

Nancy Reagan smiled for a few pictures, but she kept jiggling her leg.

"I cannot tell a lie," Dean whispered.

"What?" Clover asked.

"It's what George Washington said when he chopped down the cherry tree. Even though Gregory says that story isn't true," Ava said.

"I think Nancy Reagan is about to spill the beans."

"It's not my gerbil!" kid Nancy Reagan said. "I . . . I . . . found him."

President Abbey frowned. "But if he isn't yours, then who brought him?"

This was the moment when everything should have fallen apart. The president should have figured out that no one brought the rodent. She should have figured out that the rodent actually lived there! And then someone should have pointed out that Gregory was actually a mouse, and where there was one mouse, there were more! And then the whole Squeakerton colony should have fallen apart. Right now. Unless . . .

"He's mine!" Macey set Clover down. She stepped forward and gently took Gregory from Nancy Reagan.

The reporters swiveled to face her. Lights flashed, and cameras clicked.

"Um, he's mine, Mom," Macey said softly.

President Abbey blinked. "You have a pet gerbil? When did this happen?"

"Look." Macey leaned in to whisper. "Can Banks and I talk to you for a minute?"

"Of course." President Abbey waved at the crowd and said, "Students, there are treats in the Green Room. Please enjoy, and happy Presidents' Day."

President Abbey led her children to the Blue Room, an oval-shaped room down the hall. Clover followed. Ava and Dean were still sitting on her head.

"What's going on, guys?" the president asked.

"Is that really your gerbil?" Banks asked his sister. "Where'd he get the suit?"

"I don't know where he got the suit," Macey said. "And I think he might be a mouse. But I know it's not fun being on display like that, Mom."

President Abbey cleared her throat. "Are we talking about the gerbil or you, honey?"

"Us." Banks stood up. "Mom, we don't like having our classes here! It reminds everyone that we're the president's kids."

"Well, honey, you *are* my kids," President Abbey said.

"We know," Macey said. "But this is also our home, and it's weird having our picture taken all the time."

"And taking a field trip to our kitchen," Banks added.

"I see," President Abbey said. "Anything else?"

"We just want to be normal," Banks said.

"Or sort of normal," Macey said. "As normal as we can be."

"And friends," Banks said. "We want to make friends. Friends who like us for who we are."

"And don't care about your job," Macey finished.

There are lots of human kids out there who dream about living in the White House. They dream about meeting famous people and being a part of history. But they don't realize there are challenges too. Ava and Dean understood those feelings. After all, the Squeakerton children were kind of famous. For mice.

"It was probably hard for you to tell me that. Come give me a hug." President Abbey hugged her children. Clover rubbed her owner's leg and purred.

President Abbey dried her eyes. "I can get

everyone to leave right away. But what about this gerbil? We don't want Clover to eat him."

Clover sounded like she might choke up a hairball, but she was probably gagging at the idea of eating a mouse.

"There are a couple of mice around here," Banks said.

"What?" The president hopped onto a couch. Sheesh. Humans.

"They must live outside," Macey assured her mom. "So let's go release him in the garden."

The Abbeys returned to the reception. They were good hosts. They smiled and laughed and talked and waited until everyone left. Then they walked onto the back porch to release Gregory.

"I still don't know how he got that suit," President Abbey said.

"It's the White House, Mom," Banks said. "Sometimes things are just fancy and you don't ask questions."

They set Gregory onto the ground. Finally, he was smart enough to do something mice are very good at doing.

Running away.

9

Clover waited until the Abbeys had gone upstairs before she met Gregory outside. Ava and Dean slipped out from under the wig and waved to Gregory.

Gregory was against the White House wall. He was breathing very deeply. Ava and Dean were worried he was going to cry or yell or maybe explode.

Instead, he laughed. "Did you see that? *Did you see that?*"

"See what, Gregory?" Ava asked slowly.

"I just met the president of the United States?

Me! Gregory Squeakerton. And even though she thought I was a gerbil, which I do not want to talk about, she was still so kind! And smart! And presidential." Gregory removed his stove-pipe hat. "It's the best birthday surprise ever."

"It would have been better if you could have found the Abbey kids some friends," Clover said. "Did you hear them talking to their mom? I think they're lonely."

"Do you . . . do you care about the kids?" Ava asked, surprised.

"Happy kids means more snacks for me," Clover said. But the mice didn't really believe that. Clover had a soft side too.

Dean grabbed Gregory's claw. "Can you come with us? For real this time?"

Gregory brushed off his suit and readjusted his bow tie. "Sure. I could use a nap after all that excitement."

The mice hopped back up the stairs of the porch. Clover followed. Gregory stopped and turned around slowly. "Why is the c-a-t following us?"

Ava sighed. "That c-a-t helped us save you. So we made a deal with Clover. We can explain in a bit. Just . . . go."

Gregory kept looking over his shoulder at Clover. Clover licked her lips, which didn't help much.

Finally, at the door of the Treasure Rooms, they stopped.

"The c-a-t won't fit in here," Gregory said.

"I can understand you, you know," Clover said.

"I can't believe you speak Mouse." Gregory frowned. "Just don't eat us."

"I don't eat gerbil." Clover smiled.

"Clover, we would bring you in but . . . ," Ava said.

Clover waved a paw. "I don't want to go to your stupid party. Just get me my cake, and everyone will be happy."

"Clover!" Dean said. "Shhh!"

"What party?" Gregory asked.

Ava and Dean were again reminded it was hard to throw a surprise party. *Super* hard.

Ava and Dean pushed Gregory into the main hall of the Treasure Rooms.

"Surprise!" the Squeakerton mice cheered. Balloons bounced around the room.

And then Gregory, the big, strong mouse, fainted.

Libby waved some blue cheese under his nose to wake him up. Gregory rubbed his eyes. "I don't understand."

By this point, the Squeakerton mice were already partying. They'd waited long enough. Sullivan had set up the Wheel, so all the teenagers were running around on that. There was a photo booth with little cardboard cutouts of different presidents. Someone wrote questions about US presidents on paper along the wall, and there was a prize for whoever answered the most questions correctly.

And there was cake. One large cupcake. Carrot, actually.

"This is your surprise birthday party," Ava said. "We've been planning it for months."

"And that suit is your present," Dean said. "Sullivan said there is a sword sewn into your pants. I don't know why."

Gregory wrapped the Squeakerton kids in a hug. "It's wonderful. All of it. Thank you, little mice. I can't wait to eat some of that cake."

"About that," Ava said. "We have to give the cupcake to Clover. It was part of the trade."

"How sad," Gregory said. "I love carrot cake."

"Me too," Ava said. "So much. So, so, so much. I wish we could give Clover something else instead of cake."

"Maybe we can," Dean said. "Maybe we should ask."

It couldn't hurt. Clover seemed less scary once they knew she wouldn't eat them.

"I have an idea," Dean said. "I'll be right back."

Dean ran into another Treasure Room. He was gone for a while. Ava eyed the carrot cupcake. She really wanted that cupcake.

"Okay, sister. Let's go. I think I found another way to make Clover happy."

They met Clover outside the mouse hole.

"Hey, where's my cake?" Clover asked.

"We have something better than cake," Dean said.

"What could possibly be better than cake?" Clover asked.

Dean smiled. "That's easy. Friendship."

This time, the mice didn't have to travel in the mouse tunnels. They didn't have to sneak around the White House. With Clover (and Clover's wig), they could walk through any hallway. They could walk right up to the kids' bedrooms.

"Thanks for helping us, Clover," Ava said.

"I'm not helping you," Clover said. "I'm helping my owners!"

"You are a nice c-a-t," Dean said. "You don't fool us."

"Whatever." Clover yawned. "You still owe me a cupcake."

"Here we go." Ava and Dean held tails. Then they jumped out from under the wig and ran right into Macey's bedroom.

Macey screamed when she first saw them. The mice couldn't blame her. It *was* a surprise to have two mice run into your bedroom.

"You scared me!" she said. Then she kneeled down by the mice. "Banks! Come in here! You'll want to see this."

Ava waved at Macey again. Waving is a friendly thing to do.

"Why are they wearing green berets?" Banks asked. "Look, they have on little backpacks too."

"I don't know," Macey said. "Maybe some mice wear clothes?"

The reason mice wear clothes is because they

want to. Why do humans think mouse clothes are so strange?

Dean tipped his hat. He pulled out a piece of paper and handed it to Macey.

She unrolled the paper.

Dear Macey and Banks,

Hi! Our names are Ava and Dean. We're mice. Obviously. We know it can be fun but hard to live in the White House.

Will you be our friends? Check

YES ☐

NO ☐

Thanks for not telling anyone that we live here.

Ava and Dean Squeakerton

P.S. Gregory was very excited to meet your mom today.

P.P.S. Clover is actually very nice, but pretend like you don't know that.

"Friends? Us?" Banks looked at Clover. "Did you bring them in here because you heard us talking to Mom?"

Clover meowed. Banks grabbed his cat and cuddled her so hard that her wig fell off.

Macey smiled. She walked over to her night-stand and searched for a pen. Then she marked a big red X in the yes box.

"Thank you," she said. "We're honored."

Ava and Dean bowed. They would have shaken hands, but humans have such big hands.

Banks and Macey laughed and waved. The deal was done.

"Well, new friends," Banks said, "we were just about to head to the kitchen and eat some cupcakes. Would you like to join us?"

Ava couldn't believe her luck! Friendship *and* cupcakes!

Ava and Dean hopped into Macey's pocket.
Clover followed right behind.

And then all five of them feasted on cupcakes.

Carrot. Their favorite.

Presidential Birthdays

George Washington
February 22, 1732

John Adams
October 30, 1735

Thomas Jefferson
April 13, 1743

James Madison
March 16, 1751

James Monroe
April 28, 1758

John Quincy Adams
June 11, 1767

Andrew Jackson
March 15, 1767

Martin Van Buren
December 5, 1782

William Henry
Harrison
February 9, 1773

John Tyler
March 29, 1790

James K. Polk
November 2, 1795

Zachary Taylor
November 24, 1784

Millard Fillmore
January 7, 1800

Franklin Pierce
November 23, 1804

James Buchanan
April 23, 1791

Abraham Lincoln
February 12, 1809

Andrew Johnson
December 29, 1808

Ulysses S. Grant
April 27, 1822

Rutherford B. Hayes
October 4, 1822

James Garfield
November 19, 1831

Chester A. Arthur
October 5, 1829

Grover Cleveland
March 18, 1837

Benjamin Harrison
August 20, 1833

Grover Cleveland
March 18, 1837

William McKinley
January 29, 1843

Theodore Roosevelt
October 27, 1858

William Howard Taft
September 15, 1857

Woodrow Wilson
December 28, 1856

Warren G. Harding
November 2, 1865

Calvin Coolidge
July 4, 1872

Herbert Hoover
August 10, 1874

Franklin D. Roosevelt
January 30, 1882

Harry S. Truman
May 8, 1884

Dwight D.
Eisenhower
October 14, 1890

John F. Kennedy
May 29, 1917

Lyndon B. Johnson
August 27, 1908

Richard M. Nixon
January 9, 1913

Gerald R. Ford
July 14, 1913

James "Jimmy"
Carter
October 1, 1924

Ronald Reagan
February 6, 1911

George H. W. Bush
June 12, 1924

William J. "Bill"
Clinton
August 19, 1946

George W. Bush
July 6, 1946

Barack Obama
August 4, 1961

October is busy!
SIX presidential
birthdays!

Mice Are Smart!
Three Totally Fun Facts
About Presidential Birthdays

Even the Big Cheese deserves a big party!

1. In 1995, then–First Lady Hillary Clinton threw a Dolly Parton–themed hoedown in the White House! There were about 150 guests, and Hillary celebrated her forty-eighth birthday with square dancing and a barn-shaped birthday cake!

2. On Franklin Roosevelt's fifty-second birthday, 100,000 telegrams arrived at the White

House. One telegram was 1,280 feet long and signed by 40,000 people. It took two messengers two days to carry it to the White House!

3. President Ronald Reagan had two birthday surprises. In 1981, he had a party with lobster, dancing, and twelve cakes! In 1983, his wife, Nancy, surprised him with a cake at a press conference that was on television.

Presidents' Day

Guess what! Presidents' Day was created to celebrate George Washington's birthday, but we never celebrate it on *either* of his birthdays. That's right—George Washington has twice as many birthdays as you do!

George Washington was born on February 11, 1732, in Virginia. But then Britain and the colonies changed their calendar system, so his birthday was moved to February 22. For many decades, Presidents' Day was celebrated on his second birthday, February 22.

About fifty years ago, the holiday changed when Congress passed a law to give Americans more three-day weekends. Presidents' Day moved to the third Monday in February. But neither of George Washington's birthdays will ever fall on the third Monday of February. So even though Presidents' Day was made to celebrate George Washington's birth, the party never happens on his birthday!

The holiday is still officially called Washington's Birthday by the federal government, though many states call it Presidents' Day to include Abraham Lincoln's birthday, February 12, as part of the celebration. This holiday is a great opportunity to learn about the presidents past and present.

Clothes of the Past

★ **Shoes:** In the days of our Founding Fathers, shoes weren't very comfy! Back then, shoes were not made to curve like the human foot. Instead, they were built flat and straight, making them very uncomfortable to walk in. They also had buckles, like a belt, instead of laces!

★ **Powdered Wigs:** Powdered wigs were commonly worn in colonial times as a symbol of class and status. Wigs became fashionable when King Louis XIII, the king of France, started wearing one to cover his bald spot. The very first powdered wigs were made of horsehair. They were never washed properly, so they smelled gross and tended to attract lice. Yuck!

tricorne hat
powdered wig
breeches

★ **Breeches:** Instead of wearing full-length pants, the Founding Fathers wore breeches, pants that stopped at the knee and were fastened with buttons or drawstrings.

★ **Stockings:** Beneath their breeches, men wore silk or wool stockings to cover their calves and feet.

★ **Tricorne Hats:** Tricorne hats were very fashionable during the Founding Fathers' generation. These beaver fur or felt hats helped block the sun and also made rain drip down the brim and away from the face. A winning combination of an umbrella and a hat!

Clothes of the Present

★ **Jeans:** Jimmy Carter was the first president to wear jeans regularly. Since he grew up working on a farm, you could say that jeans were in his genes!

★ **Safer Clothes:** Presidents often wear bullet-resistant clothing to protect them while they are out in public. One of the most common fabrics used for bullet-resistant clothes is a material called Kevlar. If you put clay beneath Kevlar and fired a bullet, the clay would barely have a dent in it.

★ **Shoes:** A shoe company named Johnston & Murphy has been designing shoes for America's presidents since 1850. Barack Obama is such a big fan of Abraham Lincoln that Johnston & Murphy made him a modern replica of the boots they made for President Lincoln in 1861.

★ **Cardigans:** Jimmy Carter was famous for wearing cardigans, which made people feel like he was a humble president who could understand his citizens.

★ **First Lady Gowns:** Helen Taft, who became First Lady in 1909, started the tradition of First Ladies selecting their inaugural gown and donating it to the Smithsonian's First Ladies Collection. Now the Smithsonian has collected over two hundred years' worth of First Ladies' gowns.

Inaugural gown worn by
Lady Bird Johnson

New friends. New adventures.
Find a new series . . . just for you!

BALLPARK Mysteries
FOR THE SPORTS FAN

THE DINO FILES
FOR THE ADVENTURER

Louise Trapeze
FOR THE SUPERSTAR

PIPER GREEN
FOR THE DREAMER

PUPPY PIRATES
FOR THE ANIMAL LOVER

Totally True adventures!
FOR THE EXPLORER

Illustrations (from left to right) : © Mark Meyers; © Mike Boldt; © Brigette Barrager; © Qin Leng; © Russ Cox; © Wesley Lowe

RandomHouseKids.com